Rosie Plants a Radish

a Radish

A lift-the-flap book

Axel Scheffler

Kate Petty

MACMILLAN CHILDREN'S BOOKS

First published in paperback in 2000
First published in 1997 by Macmillan Children's Books
a division of Macmillan Publishers Limited
20 New Wharf Road, London N1 9RR
Basingstoke and Oxford
Associated companies worldwide

www.panmacmillan.com

ISBN 0 333 78107 4

3 5 7 9 8 6 4

A CIP catalogue record for this book is
available from the British Library.

Printed in China

Rosie loved radishes.

"If I had a wish," said Rosie, "I'd wish for as many radishes as I could eat."

"Why don't you plant some, then?" said Worm.

Rosie bought a packet
of radish seeds.

But when she opened it she was disappointed.
"These don't look like radishes," said Rosie.
"Radishes aren't small and brown."

Plant the seeds
Rosie, and wait
and see.

"Can I plant them on top of my burrow?" she asked.
"No," said Ladybird.
"It's too windy."

"Can I plant them under the big tree?"
"No," said Worm.
"It's too dark."

"How about this sunny spot over here?"
"Yes," said Worm and Ladybird together. "Perfect."

Rosie cleared away the grass and weeds to make
a radish patch. Then she made some shallow holes.

She put one seed in each hole, covered them up and
sprinkled them with water from her watering can.

For two days Rosie watched and
waited for her radishes to grow.
"I knew it wouldn't work,"
said Rosie sadly.

But the next day, Ladybird had news for Rosie.
"The radishes are growing, Rosie. Come and look."

"Humph," said Rosie. "They don't look like radishes.
Radishes aren't small and green."

The next day the sun shone.
It warmed the ground.
It warmed Rosie.
It warmed the little radish shoots.

At teatime Rosie felt hungry.
So she went to look at her
radish patch – just in case.

It was full of little plants.

"They've grown a lot today," said Rosie.
"But they still don't look like radishes.
Radishes aren't green and leafy."

But then it rained.
"Horrid rain, ruining my radishes,"
moaned Rosie. "Ladybird said they
needed sunshine."

"But they need water too," said Worm.
"Let's go and look at your book."

"These roots don't look like a radish," said Rosie crossly.
"Radishes aren't long and hairy!"

 Rosie looked at her radishes every day.

She weeded them  and watered them.

The radishes grew

and grew

and grew!

And below the ground the radishes grew...

bigger

and rounder

and redder.

"Do they look like radishes yet?" asked Rosie.
"Have a look, Rosie!" said Ladybird.

So Rosie pulled

and pulled

and pulled

and out popped...

a radish!

"It looks like a radish now," said Rosie.
"And it tastes like a radish, too."

HOW TO GROW RADISH SEEDS

Here are some of our gardening tips.

Buy some good quality radish seeds from your local garden centre.

You can plant the radish seeds outside in spring and summer.

You can also plant them in pots on a windowsill or balcony, or indoors, if you want to start them a little earlier in the year.

Plant the seeds in garden soil or potting compost.

Plant the seeds 5 centimetres apart and 1 centimetre deep.

Water regularly, making sure that the soil doesn't dry out.

They take about three weeks to grow.

It is actually quite difficult to use seeds from your own radishes. You will get better results if you buy the seeds each year.

Have fun!

Enjoy your radishes!